Tiger Lily

A Heroine in the Making!

STRIPES PUBLISHING
An imprint of Magi Publications
1 The Coda Centre, 189 Munster Road, London SW6 6AW

A paperback original
First published in Great Britain in 2007

Text copyright © Maeve Friel, 2007
Illustrations copyright © Joelle Dreidemy, 2007

The right of Maeve Friel and Joelle Dreidemy to be identified as the
author and illustrator of this work has been asserted by them in
accordance with the Copyright, Designs and Patents Act, 1988.

ISBN: 978 1 84715 019 6

A CIP catalogue record for this book is available from the British
Library.

Printed and bound in the UK

10 9 8 7 6 5 4 3

A Heroine in the Making!

Maeve Friel

Illustrated by
Joelle Dreidemy

Stripes

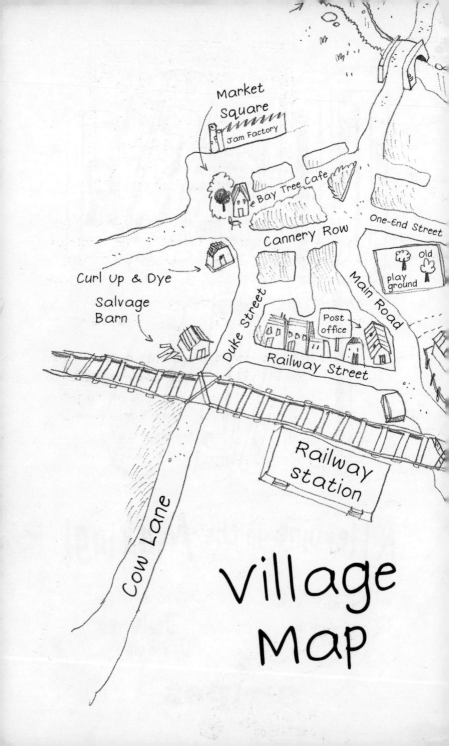

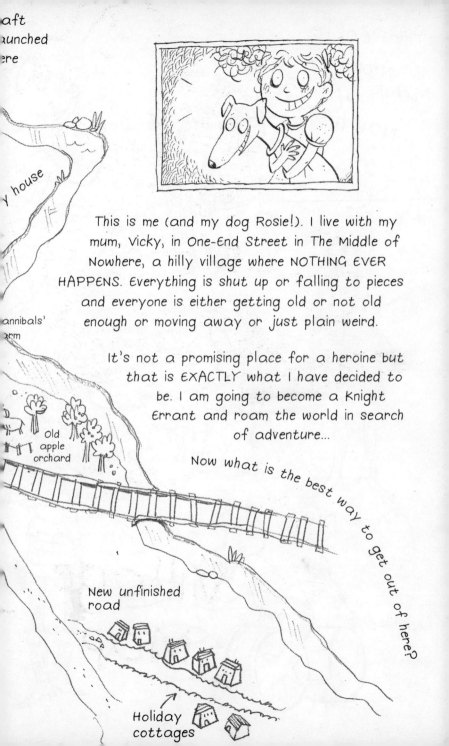

aft
unched
ere

y house

annibals'
arm

old
apple
orchard

This is me (and my dog Rosie!). I live with my mum, Vicky, in One-End Street in The Middle of Nowhere, a hilly village where NOTHING EVER HAPPENS. Everything is shut up or falling to pieces and everyone is either getting old or not old enough or moving away or just plain weird.

It's not a promising place for a heroine but that is EXACTLY what I have decided to be. I am going to become a Knight Errant and roam the world in search of adventure...

Now what is the best way to get out of here?

New unfinished road

Holiday cottages

Sweetness and Light, the Misses Wolf

Auntie Pamela of Curl Up & Dye

Streaky Bacon Junior

Milo

Spanners Murphy, the plumber

Mr & Mrs Hannibal

Chapter 1

"Lily! Lily! For the last time! LILY!" Mum roared from the bottom of the stairs.

Lily did not hear her mother shouting. That was because only her mother called Lily *Lily*: everyone else called her Tiger. But the main reason she didn't hear anything was because she had her nose stuck in a book.

All her life Tiger Lily had been mad about books. Her house on One-End Street was STUFFED with them. As well as the books on the bookshelves, there were

books in the bedrooms, books in the hall, books in the bathroom, books in the kitchen and books on the stairs. There were books on tables and under tables, books on chairs and between chairs and behind chairs. There were even books under the stairs along with the Christmas decorations and an inflatable giraffe. The whole house was suffering from a bad case of BOOK CREEP. Books were taking over every single empty space. And where there were no books, there were poems. Tiger Lily Sellotaped them to doors and walls. She even stuck a bit of her favourite poem, *The Pied Piper of Hamelin,* on the fridge under two magnets.

10

"So munch on, crunch on,
take your nuncheon,
Breakfast, supper,
dinner, luncheon!"

Tiger Lily's mother, Vicky, loved books too. She drove the mobile library van and sometimes took Lily with her when she went on her rounds of all the little villages in their valley. Everywhere they went, there were people with their noses stuck in books. The library van regulars liked romances and detective stories. The hill walkers carried slim volumes of poetry in their rucksacks. The summer visitors snoozed on the beach with thick paperbacks rising and falling on their tummies.

But Tiger was more than just fond of reading: she was OBSESSED!

She had read how Fern had rescued the little pig Wilbur from her father's axe in *Charlotte's Web*.

She was green with envy that Alice had followed the White Rabbit down the rabbit-hole and found herself in Wonderland.

Sometimes, she wished that she could have a monkey like Pippi Longstocking, and live alone in a cottage where she could do exactly what she wanted when she wanted.

At other times, she longed to find a mysterious cousin in the attic like the girl in *The Secret Garden*.

But best of all, she wished that she could be like Jo March in *Little Women*, and sell her beautiful chestnut hair (if only she had beautiful chestnut hair) to save her family from certain ruin. (Which was what was going to happen if her mum didn't pass her driving test for the big new-style library vans.)

All this reading had gone to Tiger's head. It was always giving her ingenious ideas, and it had got her into trouble *countless* times before – like the time when she had dug up the garden looking for jewels after reading *The Treasure Seekers*. But she had forgotten all that when, on the first Saturday of the half-term holiday, she made up her mind that she too would be a HEROINE.

But which sort of heroine could she be? What was the best way to go about it?

She turned over a new leaf in her notebook and drew up a list.

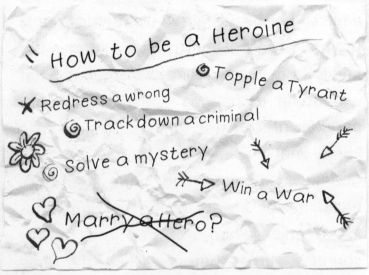

How to be a Heroine

✗ Redress a wrong

⊚ Topple a Tyrant

⊚ Track down a criminal

⊚ Solve a mystery

❥ Win a War

♡ Marry a Hero?

Any of these would do except for the last one. She wanted to be a heroine in her own right, not a wishy-washy princess, and anyway she didn't intend to marry anyone for a very long time. She scratched out the last entry and looked at the list again.

There was still a problem. Since absolutely nothing ever happened in The Middle of Nowhere, she would have to go a-roaming in search of adventures. But how could she go a-roaming when she didn't have a horse? Or a hot-air balloon or a broomstick, a carriage or a man-o'-war? She didn't even have a bicycle.

And there was another problem. Every heroine needs a companion – a squire or a wise fairy or devoted slave; a family of younger brothers and sisters might have done except that she didn't have any...

There wasn't even anybody her age in the village now that her best friend Sammy had moved to the city. There was only Milo Hannibal and his gang and the little wieners at the Mothers and Toddlers' Group.

She was lying on her bed, wondering where on earth she could find a TRUSTY DEVOTED companion, the kind that would stop at nothing, who would even lay down their life for her if the need arose, when…

"LILY!"

Tiger Lily was so shocked by the sudden appearance of her mother looming over her in a bright red puffa jacket that she jumped off the bed, upset a pile of books and accidentally stood on Rosie, who started barking unhelpfully. (Rosie was a nervous and very skinny three-legged greyhound that Lily had rescued from under the railway bridge a few days earlier.)

TIGERLILY

"Lily, didn't you hear me shouting? We're really late. We've got to go NOW! I've got a driving lesson and then a meeting with my Awful Boss and after that I'm going to Auntie Pamela's to get my hair done. Come on! Hurry Up!"

As usual, Tiger Lily thought that her mum was far too bright. Her clothes were too colourful – canary yellow boots! flowery skirt! spearmint leggings! – and she had far, far too much frizzy hair that fell around her shoulders in hundreds of little corkscrews. Personally, Lily would have preferred a quieter, duller mum – one like Marmee in *Little Women*, instead of The Red Queen from *Alice*.

"Do you know," she

mused, holding Rosie's jaws clamped shut with both hands to stop the yowling, "there are hardly any mums in books. Pippi Longstocking doesn't have a mum and neither does Alice; and Mary Lennox, the girl from *The Secret Garden*, was an orphan and so was that girl who went up the Amazon with her governess..."

Mum burst out laughing. "So you'd like to get rid of me too, is that what you're saying? Honestly, Lily!"

She dropped a quick kiss on the top of Lily's head. "If you hurry up, I'll take you round to Granny's. Or do you want to stay with Auntie Pamela at Curl Up & Dye?"

But Tiger Lily wasn't listening. She was steering her canoe through river channels choked with mangrove roots, heading for a magical opera house in the middle of the Amazonian rainforest.

"LILY! You're miles away. Stop daydreaming. We have to go NOW!"

And her mum set off across the living room, skilfully slaloming around the piles of books on the floor. "By the way," she shouted over her shoulder, "we need to talk about that dog. You must find a home for it before you go back to school."

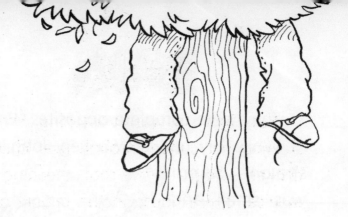

Chapter 2

As soon as Tiger Lily got out of the car at the corner of Market Square, the bay tree outside Granny Rita's café spoke to her.

"Hello, Tiger," it said.

She spun around. Dangling from beneath the round cap of glossy leaves was a pair of familiar legs.

"Sammy? Is that you?" Tiger Lily's eyes lit up. "Why didn't you email to say you were coming?"

Sammy and Tiger had been best friends until he and his mum went to live in the city.

They were complete opposites.

While Lily had grown very long and straight, Sammy was small and barrel-shaped. She had two springy bunches of stripy carroty hair; he had short black stubbly hair shaved close to his head. Tiger wanted to reform the world and was full of Big Ideas: Sammy was down to earth and full of common sense.

Tiger Lily read non-stop.

Sammy never *ever* read if he could possibly help it — his best thing was playing the drums when he came to stay with his dad during the holidays.

And now even their dogs were opposites. Rosie was so skinny and transparent you could see her ribs. Sammy's dog, Zog, was a round fat spaniel with long curly-haired ginger ears that almost reached the ground. (Sammy pinned them back with a clothes peg when he fed him so that they wouldn't get covered in dog food gloop.)

TIGERLILY

Tiger Lily was just climbing up into the tree to tell Sammy her new plan about becoming a heroine when there was a furious banging on the picture window of the Bay Tree Café and her granny shot out of the door, brandishing a ladle.

"STREAKY!"

she roared. "Leave my tables alone!"

Mr Bacon, known to everyone as Streaky, was the builder who was restoring the Old Jam Factory, which took up the topside of the square. A sun-bleached banner, splattered with

pigeon poo, hung limply between its second-floor windows – you could just about make out the words: Community Centre Opening Soon.

The work had been dragging on for so long without an end in sight that Granny and Streaky had declared out-and-out war.

She had had enough of the hammering and the dust and the scaffolding and the skips and the lorries turning around and the spilt bags of sand and the cement mixers that rumbled from morning to night.

Streaky had had enough of Granny.

That morning, she had put out the café's outdoor tables in the middle of the square so Streaky couldn't get past with his forklift truck to deliver a pallet load of blocks. To make matters worse, it was bin day, so the pavements were piled high with bin bags and a huge cardboard box that the café's new freezer had come in.

Tiger Lily and Sammy giggled as Streaky guiltily sprang away from Granny and her lethal ladle.

Streaky was so round he was almost spherical. In his orange high-visibility jacket he was like a giant space-hopper with fly-away eyebrows and a hard hat.

"Please let me move these tables aside, Rita. It won't take five minutes."

"Why didn't you make your deliveries

earlier. You're a menace to my customers."

"What customers?"

Streaky spread his arms wide to demonstrate the empty square.

Granny Rita gave him a very hard stare.

"Just out of interest," she said, flicking a scornful eyebrow at the 'Opening Soon' banner, "how soon is 'Soon'?"

Then, without waiting for a reply, she turned on her heel and click-clacked back into the café on her high heels. As she passed the tree, she whispered, "Good morning, Tiger. Good morning, Sammy."

27

Tiger Lily rolled her eyes. Grannies in books had currant-bun faces. They liked knitting. They didn't wear high heels and lipstick.

She pushed Sammy over on the branch. "You've come back just in time," she told him. "I have a plan. I have decided to be a heroine. I'm going to roam the world like a Knight Errant in search of adventure as soon as I've worked out how to get out of here. Will you be my trusty companion and come with me?" Sammy pointed one of his wooden pistols at a starling that had landed on Streaky's pallet. "Do you mean you're

running away from home?"

"No! I have to be here when Mum gets back at half past one."

"Would you pay me?"

"No."

"That's a pity 'cause what I need, Tiger, is a mobile phone and a new snare drum."

Tiger Lily sighed. This was not the way the heroine's companion behaved in books. She glumly watched the starling pecking at the plastic wrapping of the building blocks.

Then she had one of her ingenious ideas. "Come on," she said, dropping down from the tree. "Let's visit your dad."

And before Sammy could answer, she set off at a run down Duke Street with Rosie bouncing along beside her on her three legs.

For a few seconds Sammy dithered – Tiger Lily's ideas were always landing him in trouble with his dad – but, on the other hand, what could go wrong if it had something *to do* with his dad?

"Wait for me," he shouted and slithered down from the branch.

Zog waddled behind him with his ears sweeping the ground.

Chapter 3

Sammy's dad was Nick the Chippie. He worked in a big barn crammed with wooden stuff and when he wasn't down the river fishing, he spent his days planing, sawing, carving, staining, varnishing and fixing wood.

Tiger Lily thought that the Salvage Barn was one of the best places in the village. It was full of old doors and window frames, table legs and chair backs, roof beams and railway sleepers, wardrobes and cartwheels, the front half of an old boat, a pony trap,

picture frames, fishing rods and, in one corner, Nick and Sammy's sets of drums.

Sammy kept his drums in the barn because his mum didn't let him practice in his own house. For obvious reasons. But his dad was a really good drummer. According to Auntie Pamela, who read it in a magazine, Sammy's dad had been the drummer in Paul Mann's first band, Mann's People!

Tiger loved the way the floor of the barn was ankle-deep in little blonde curls of wood, as if a giant baby had just had its first haircut. But best of all, when Nick the Chippie was in a good mood, he would take an offcut and make her a little carving. She already had a small pig called Wilbur, a tiny doll which she named Thumbelina and a very fine walnut frog called Prince.

He had also made Sammy's pistols and two really strong wooden swords that were great for having a duel.

Today though, Nick was busy sawing and had ear protectors on so he didn't notice Sammy and Tiger running through the workshop to the backyard.

34

Tiger Lily stopped in front of a high stack of wooden pallets.

"That's what we need."

"A pallet?"

"I was thinking," she dropped her voice, "about how to get out of here. I was thinking about Huckleberry Finn and a journey down the river. I was thinking about a RAFT."

"Tiger!" Sammy's eyes opened wide with delight.

Tiger Lily's Book Reports
As told to her trusty companion, Sammy.

Huckleberry Finn by Mark Twain

Huckleberry Finn runs away from his wicked father. Then Jim, the slave, runs away from his wicked cruel master. This book happened a long time ago in America when rich people still owned slaves. Huck and Jim meet up and take a raft and sail down the mighty Mississippi River together and have lots of adventures. Some of them are scary and some are funny.
This is a very good book for giving you ideas about journeys. Huck says:
"You feel mighty free and easy and comfortable on a raft."

If you haven't read this book, you should.

I give it: 5 rafts

They nudged a pallet off the stack with a long broom handle and, huffing and puffing, carried it (and the broom too, Tiger Lily insisted) all the way up Duke Street.

They had to scuttle past Curl Up & Dye in case Auntie Pamela was looking out of the window, and run even faster past the Bay Tree Café, but the coast was clear. Milo Hannibal and Streaky Bacon Junior were in the old playground but they were so busy trying to pull the swings out of the ground that they didn't notice the walking pallet.

At the top of Bridge Lane, they hoisted the pallet over the bridge and threw it down on to the river bank below. Then they climbed over themselves and, with Rosie and Zog barking at their ankles, hauled their raft down to the water's edge. The little green river curled away through the Hannibals' farm between stands of bamboo canes.

"On the count of three," Lily commanded Sammy, "one, two, three...

charge!"

She took off in a glorious flying tackle, throwing herself at the canes like a real tiger crashing through the jungle. "Waaaaah!"

They whooped and yelled and stomped and soon had flattened out a big enough gap where they could launch the raft.

"Now," Tiger said, sliding the pallet into the water, "don't forget, I am Huckleberry Finn..."

"Wait a minute. If you want to be a heroine, shouldn't you pick a girl story?"

"No," said Tiger Lily, shaking her head, "I can be anyone I want. And you are the runaway slave, Jim."

Sammy's jaw dropped. "You can be anyone you want but I'm a SLAVE?"

"Yes, but you love me. You call me *honey child*."

"Honey child?" Sammy hooted.

"That's what it says in the book, silly!" Lily said, rolling her eyes. "Now jump on. Come on, Rosie, come on Zog."

The pallet rocked a bit under their weight. Then little by little, in slow motion, it began to sink. The water splashed around their feet. It seeped into their shoes. It lapped around their ankles in a ticklish sort of way.

Rosie gave a yelp and leaped off.

Zog belly-flopped after her.

The raft gave a final wobble and sank to the bottom of the stony riverbed, leaving Tiger Lily and Sammy standing up to their knees in water.

"Jim, we have a problem," said Tiger.

"Yes, *honey child*, we're shipwrecked and we haven't even set sail," said Sammy.

They scrambled off and hauled the pallet back up on to the bank.

Sammy pulled off his shoes to wring out his socks. "Do you want to go back to my dad's and listen to me play my drums?"

"No, thank you," Lily replied, politely. "I'm going to fix this raft." She had a steely glint in her eye. "I just need something to help it float."

While Sammy squeezed the water out of Zog's ears, Tiger Lily thought hard about flotation devices.

41

"Ah-ha!" she jumped up. "I have an idea! See you back here in half an hour. You go home and get some provisions for our trip, stuff like candles and ship's biscuits and grog – that's what sailors drink."

"Forget candles!" Sammy said. "I'll just get loads of biscuits and grog."

"And don't forget, my trusty companion, this is a Top Secret mission."

Once again, a shadow of doubt flickered across Sammy's face – but just for a moment. After all, Tiger had promised that they would be back by lunchtime.

Chapter 4

As usual, the village streets were deserted. Tiger Lily would not have been surprised to see a huge round ball of tumbleweed rolling towards her.

In the Bay Tree Café, Streaky Bacon and Spanners Murphy, the plumber, were watching dog racing on the television.

Granny Rita was behind the counter, making her legendary bean soup for lunch. She hardly looked up when Tiger Lily rushed in and asked if she could 'borrow' a large bin liner.

"Help yourself, Tiger," she said, "but tell Pam to buy her own bin liners. Is she very busy this morning? Would you like some toast?"

Tiger Lily scarpered before she had to answer any of the questions.

Five minutes later, she was just leaving the square with the now-bulging bin liner when she collided with the Wolf twins, Sweetness and Light.

Sweetness and Light were anything but sweet or light by nature. In fact, they always looked as if they were on the point of blowing their tops. Their real names were Sophia (pronounced So-FIE-a) and Lydia, and they lived in the Post Office & General Stores. (Hardly anyone ever shopped there any more but they still had a shop sign over their front door and opened up every day.)

Even though the Wolf twins were *ancient*, they were still identical. They had the same grey eyes, the same thin lips – and noses that were sharp enough to cut cheese. When they were out and about, they wore matching wasp-waisted grey coats, ankle boots and black velvet berets; the kind of clothes Mary Poppins might have worn.

In the shop they kept their hats on and wore frilly aprons that they sewed themselves. They were good at sewing. Sometimes Mum asked them to fix broken zips or sew on buttons.

Tiger Lily could never tell them apart.

"Ooops," she apologized, picking up Sweetness's beret and a stray orange that had fallen out of Light's basket (or possibly, Light's beret and Sweetness's basket). "Terribly sorry. Are you both all right?"

TIGERLILY

Sweetness and Light looked down their long sharp noses and pursed their thin lips. They narrowed their eyes. Sweetness, or possibly Light, put her beret back on. They opened their mouths but snapped them shut again without speaking. They eyed the bin liner with its bulging contents. Then they turned sharply on their heels and marched off, pointy elbows click-clacking like pistons. Could they be witches? Tiger wondered. Or aliens? A pair of crows that had somehow taken on human form? Or a pair of wolves dressed up as grannies?

Tiger hurried on. There was one other thing she needed to find in the cupboard under the stairs.

By the time Sammy returned to the river bank, Tiger Lily looked as if she had been dragged through a hedge backwards, but she had solved the floating problem.

"Look, I took all the pieces of polystyrene from the box that Granny's new freezer came in and stuffed them between the two wooden layers of the pallet."

"Will that work?" said Sammy, doubtfully.

"Of course it will work. Did you get the biscuits?"

Sammy proudly unpacked his provisions. "Biscuits for us and biscuits for dogs. A chicken leg. Two apples. Grog. What did you get?"

Tiger Lily rummaged in her bin liner. "One old towel."

"What's that for?"

"You'll see. A ship's logbook, a pen and…" With a great flourish, Tiger pulled out a deflated green plastic giraffe.

"This is Gerry, my beach giraffe. He'll help float the raft too."

"Tiger, you're ingenious!" Sammy made a drum roll with the chicken leg on the pallet.

Then they set to work inflating Gerry and attached his spindly back legs to the front of the raft with strips of bin liner.

"Now, it's like one of those old sailing ships with a mermaid or a monster at the front," said Sammy, admiringly.

Tiger Lily frowned. "But then we can't be Huckleberry Finn and Jim going down the Mississippi on a raft."

"That's fine by me," said Sammy. "I didn't want to be a slave anyway. And I won't have to call you *honey child*."

"We'd better be vikings or pirates then."

"Pirates," Sammy answered immediately. "I'm not wearing a stupid helmet with horns like those cows on the Hannibals' farm."

Tiger Lily was very pleased with the way her roaming was turning out so far. She drew a skull and crossbones on the towel, tied it to a stick of bamboo and poked it into a gap in the pallet. Then, after Sammy had persuaded Rosie and Zog aboard again with a trail of broken dog biscuits, she unscrewed the broom from its handle.

"There!" she said, pushing off from the bank. "A pole for punting!"

The water lapped around them. They pressed their feet hard against the wood to steady themselves. They held their breath. Then a little eddy lifted them bumpily out into the middle of the stream.

They were OFF!

Tiger Lily sat with her back against the flagpole and made her first entry in her ship's log.

Captain's Log
May 22nd

09:30   Coast clear for roaming.
Captain and Trusty Companion
launched the raft from the Bridge.
It sank.

10:00   Redesigned raft. Stocked up
on provisions. Put up Gerry Giraffe.

10:30   Relaunched. Raft floated.

"I've renamed our ship the *Hispaniola*,"
she said after a bit.

"Why's that?" said Sammy, with a stricken
look on his face. "What's the story now?"

"*Treasure Island*. It's the best pirate
book ever. I'm Long John Silver, the
pirate, and we are looking for buried
treasure on Skeleton Island. I have a parrot
and a wooden leg."

"What do I have?"

"You don't have anything. You're Jim Hawkins, the wretched cabin boy."

"Another *Jim*? And now I am *wretched*?" Sammy objected.

"Yes," said Tiger Lily. "From now on, I will call you 'me hearty' and you say 'Ahoy there, cap'n' when you want to speak."

"Why?" asked Sammy, wondering if all wannabe heroines were as bossy to their trusty companions as Tiger Lily.

"Because that is what happens in the book. Shiver me timbers, me hearty, I told you that you have to do it like it says in the book."

"Hmmm," said Sammy.

Tiger Lily's Book Reports
As told to her trusty companion, Sammy.

Treasure Island by R.L. Stevenson

This is a very exciting book especially if you like
adventure stories, particularly ones about pirates.
It is all about a boy called Jim Hawkins, that's you,
who finds a pirate map and goes on an EXPEDITION
to find the buried treasure.
The cook on his ship is called Long John Silver, that's
me, but he is really a PIRATE and he plans a mutiny.
The story is a bit hard because Long John Silver
keeps switching sides and sometimes he is good to Jim
and sometimes he is sneaky.
When the pirates drink grog and fight among each
other, they give Long John Silver a BLACK SPOT –
that means he cannot be their leader any more.
After a lot of adventures, they find the treasure in
Ben Gunn's cave.
The best person in the book is Long John Silver though
he is the baddie really.

I give it: 5 treasure chests full of money and pearls

In some places, stretches of bamboo had fallen over with the wind and formed little green tunnels. That meant they had to get off, lower the flag and push the raft through. It was not easy where the water was deep and they had to wade and steer at the same time.

The worst problem was Rosie. She kept leaping off, startled by the Hannibals' peacocks screeching "Pieces of Eight", or the way the big woolly cattle stopped grazing to stare at them as they floated past. Or the bleating of the Hannibals' goats. Or the sound of splashing water. Or the shadows the bamboos cast on the raft. Everything really.

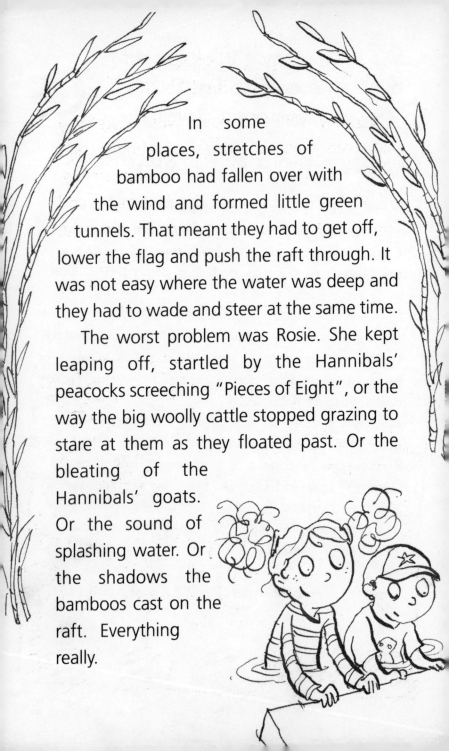

So they were all sopping wet before they had even reached the railway bridge and Tango the station cat made his appearance. Off shot Rosie. Up went the *Hispaniola* and Zog, Sammy and Tiger Lily slid into the Caribbean Sea. Sammy had to agree with Tiger Lily that there was absolutely nothing better than messing about on a river.

They were just coming out of one of the bamboo tunnels, loudly singing

"Fifteen men on a dead man's chest,
Yo-Ho-Ho and a bottle of rum,"

when Sammy stopped punting and said, "Ahoy there, cap'n. I smell something burning."

Sure enough, when they rounded the next bend, they saw smoke rising from a clearing near a small wooden jetty.

"Some pesky landlubber has seen our skull and crossbones, I daresay, Jim lad. That must be a beacon to warn the natives there are pirates on the coast." Tiger Lily made a note in her ship's log. "Drop anchor, me hearty, and take your pistols and cutlass. We're going ashore."

"Aye aye, Mr Silver, sir, cap'n. It must be time for grog anyway," said Sammy.

Captain's Log
May 22nd

10:45 Hunting party went ashore without permission to chase peacocks and nearly sank the Hispaniola.

11:00 Unauthorized hunting party went ashore again to investigate Mrs Hannibal's goats. Raft capsized. Jim Hawkins mutinous. Captain gave out ship's biscuits.

11:30 Passed through bamboo tunnels. Got soaked. Sighted Tango the station cat – cabin boy unsuccessfully sat on hunting party to prevent more unplanned shore leave. Raft capsized.

12:00 Moored the Hispaniola and went ashore to check smoke signals.

Chapter 5

They had no rope to tie up their raft so they rammed it under the jetty and set off to investigate.

They had landed beside the new Holiday Village, Streaky Bacon's other half-finished project. Five roofless cottages stood in a semicircle on a dusty patch of ground.

A man in a long yellow coat and a beanie was sitting on a small log in front of a smouldering fire, eating an apple. He had a toolbox and another narrow black case at his feet.

Tiger Lily gasped. "An escaped convict! Let's creep up on him and arrest him."

"Hang on! How can you tell? He isn't wearing one of those jail suits with arrows on them," said Sammy, sensibly.

"They don't wear those nowadays. Do you think he has a musket or a blunderbuss in that case?"

"No! Tiger, wait!" Sammy hissed, but Lily had already started to creep forward on her hands and knees. Unfortunately, the convict chose that moment to lob his apple core into the high grass. Zog immediately thought it was a game of catch and bounded out of cover with Rosie bouncing along behind her.

"Cześć! Skąd oni przyszli?"

Tiger Lily looked at Sammy and raised her eyebrows. Sammy raised his shoulders and let them drop.

"He's speaking in tongues to confuse us. We must be very careful. He may be dangerous."

"He doesn't look very dangerous," whispered Sammy. "Look, he's tickling Zog's tummy."

64

Tiger Lily stood up and whistled.

"Hey, mister," she shouted, "leave our dogs alone."

"Ah, it's the pirates!" said the man. He spoke with a strange accent. "I was watching your boat as it came around the bend!"

"Are you a spy?"

"Me?"

Tiger Lily tilted her head to one side and stroked her chin. "Maybe not. I expect that you're a convict on the run like Magwitch in *Great Expectations*, but that's OK. We can give you a chicken leg and an apple but then you have to go to Australia and become very rich and be my *benefactor*. Being a benefactor means you have to do good things for me."

"Tiger!" Sammy poked her in the ribs. "Stop it!"

Tiger Lily's Book Reports
As told to her trusty companion, Sammy.

Great Expectations by Charles Dickens

Mum is reading this to me. Pip is an orphan and he lives with his awful big sister and is nearly always starving with hunger. On Christmas Eve, on the marshes, he finds a prisoner on the run. He is called Magwitch and Magwitch scares him into giving him food and stealing a file to cut the chain off his foot. It is very scary and very exciting. There is a mad woman called Miss Havisham in the story. She was abandoned on her wedding day years ago but she still wears her wedding dress and lives in a house full of cobwebs. Pip comes into money and he thinks that Miss Havisham is his secret BENEFACTOR but his benefactor was really Magwitch who had gone to Australia and made a fortune.

I give it: 4 cobwebs

The man looked a bit confused. "My name is Piotr. I am from Poland. I don't want to go to Australia. I hoped someone here might give me a job, but whoever was burning this rubbish has gone."

"If you mean Streaky Bacon, the builder, he doesn't work here on Saturdays. He's at the Jam Factory."

Piotr was wondering if he had understood correctly that the builder made jam on Saturdays when he noticed that Sammy and Tiger Lily were both staring at his case.

He bent down to pick it up, carefully laid it on his lap, undid the catch and drew out...

"I knew it!" Sammy yelled. "It's a flute! Can you play it?"

Piotr nodded. "In my country," he said, fitting the pieces of the flute together, "I played in a small orchestra, but now I have come here to work and save some money. Would you like to hear a tune?"

As the man raised the flute to his lips, Tiger Lily noticed that around his neck, he wore a scarf with red and yellow stripes.

She could hardly believe her luck.

"It's the Pied Piper!" she whispered to Sammy. She hugged herself with pleasure. Things were looking up. "Now all we need is a plague of rats."

Tiger Lily's Book Reports
As told to her trusty companion, Sammy.

The Pied Piper by Robert Browning

This is not a book – it is a long poem.

"Come in!" the Mayor cried, looking bigger
And in did come the strangest figure!
His queer long coat from heel to head
Was half of yellow and half of red.
And he himself was tall and thin
With sharp blue eyes, each like a pin
And light loose hair, yet swarthy skin
No tuft on cheek nor beard on chin,
But lips where smiles went out and in..."

The town of Hamelin has a plague of RATS and
nobody knows what to do. Then the Pied Piper comes
and he plays his flute and leads the rats out of
the houses and into the river where they drown. But
the Mayor is greedy and won't pay the Pied Piper
his money so he plays his flute again and all the
children come out and follow him. But, don't worry,
he doesn't drown them. He leads them through a rock
in the mountain to a secret magic land. Only one boy
with a limp is left behind to tell what happens.

This is my favourite poem at the moment.
I give it: 5 rats

"I know a job you could do," Tiger Lily said when the music stopped. "You could play your flute and lead the rats out of all the cities all over the world and drown them in the rivers."

"That's an excellent suggestion," said Piotr. "I wonder where you can find out about jobs like that."

Tiger Lily wrinkled her nose. "I could ask my mum to put up an ad on the noticeboard in the City library, if you like."

PIED PIPER SEEKS WORK (OWN FLUTE)

Rat Extermination A Speciality.

GREAT With Children.

Warmly recommended by the Caliph of Baghdad and the Lord of Tartary

Fee Payable in Advance ... OR ELSE.

Ask for Piotr

Piotr smiled. "That would be very kind of you. Would you like a Polish dumpling? They're called *pierogi*."

He pulled up some breeze blocks next to the fire and Lily and Sammy sat down to dry out and share their biscuits and grog. Piotr played more tunes. Zog and Rosie lay at his feet and had a nap until somewhere, far off, a bell chimed one o'clock.

Tiger Lily jumped up.

"Oh no! We have to go. I promised Mum I'd be back at half past one – but, Piotr, I have another idea. This afternoon, Sammy and I will go to a pet shop. We'll buy up all the mice and rats and hamsters and release them in the Old Jam Factory. Then you must arrive and bow and say, 'Ladies and Gentlemen, I am the Pied Piper, Rat Catcher to European and

Asian royalty.' 'Come in, come in,' Streaky the builder will say, 'you have arrived in the nick of time. We are at our wits' ends.' And everyone will shower you with money and prizes and then you can stay and live here and teach us magic."

"And music," added Sammy.

Piotr looked at the pallet raft and the deflating giraffe figurehead.

"Where *exactly* do you have to go?" he asked.

"That's our village back there," said Tiger Lily, with an airy wave. "That's the chimney of the Old Jam Factory."

"Where the builders are working today?"

Tiger Lily nodded.

"Good," Piotr said. "Be careful with your sailing. Be very careful. I hope we will meet again very soon."

They all shook hands.

Chapter 6

Tiger Lily turned the *Hispaniola* to face homewards. They then coaxed the dogs back on board, and Tiger pushed off from the bank with the broom handle. The raft wobbled a bit and then moved swiftly off on the downstream current.

"WHOA!" she shouted. "Steer properly. We're going in the wrong direction."

"I AM steering properly. You'll have to punt faster!" Sammy shouted back.

But, of course, it was no use at all. The *Hispaniola* glided further downstream,

73

gathering speed, taking them further away from home.

"We're going to be washed out to sea," Lily wailed, poling furiously against the current.

The words were hardly out of her mouth when a sneaky gust of wind caught the skull and crossbones flag and wrapped it around her face. Blinded, she tripped over Rosie. Rosie lost her balance and both of them tumbled into the river along with the flag, the punting pole and all the provisions.

The raft, with its lighter load, speeded up. It swirled and bobbed and spun, carrying Sammy and Zog further and further downriver.

"Tiger! Help!" Sammy roared.

"Abandon ship!" Lily roared back.

Sammy wasted no time. He picked up Zog and threw himself headlong over Gerry's neck, ending up on his bottom mid-stream in a tangle of spindly green plastic, duckweed and spaniel ears. The raft sailed on.

Tiger Lily and Sammy looked at each other in silence for a long time. Then they gathered up Gerry, crawled out on to the riverbank and set off across the fields with Rosie and Zog dripping behind them.

They tramped along for ages without speaking. Lily limped like the boy shut out for ever from the magic world of the Pied Piper. Her shoes sloshed. Her nose dripped. Worst of all, the midges had come out.

"I'm being eaten alive," she fumed, scratching her hair madly.

Only Sammy was cheerful. "Why don't you pretend to be a sailor coming back from the war?" he suggested. "There must be a book about it. Pretend you have defeated the enemy and survived shipwreck. Soon the bells will be ringing out to welcome you back home." He gave a little snort and a ripple of a giggle, but quickly put on a serious face when Tiger Lily gave him a hard stare.

She wiped her nose with the back of her hand and poked at an itch between her shoulder blades. She was so furious that she didn't even notice that Rosie had bounced ahead to bark at a van that was coming straight down the path towards them.

"Toot, toot."

Chapter 7

It was the library van with Tiger Lily's mum behind the wheel and Nick the Chippie in the passenger seat. Both looked murderous.

"Going down the river on a PALLET!" her mum exploded. "I suppose this was one of your so-called ingenious ideas."

Tiger Lily stared at her mother. Her head was a concertina of dozens of flat pieces of silver foil and she was wearing a Curl Up & Dye tunic. She looked like an Egyptian.

"Mum, it was brilliant. We were pirates and we met Magwitch and gave him food…"

"…but he wasn't really Magwitch," said Sammy. "He's a fantastic musician…"

"…like the Pied Piper…"

Nick the Chippie and Tiger's mum exchanged a serious look.

"The Pied Piper? Lily, are you crazy? What have I told you about talking to strangers?"

"As for you, Sammy," said Nick the Chippie, "have you any idea the trouble you've caused? You scared us both to death."

"You could both have been drowned."

"Of all the most irresponsible…"

"…stupid…"

"…dangerous…"

"…crackpot…"

Both the grown-ups were talking loudly at the same time.

Tiger Lily and Sammy clambered up the steps into the back of the van with the two sopping dogs.

"You're grounded," Mum said. She crossly slammed the van into reverse gear and steered back up the grassy lane to the main road. "You are not to put a FOOT outside the village until I say so."

"But it's half-term," Tiger protested.

"Grounded," repeated Mum, glaring at Lily and Rosie in the rear-view mirror. "And that dog has GOT TO GO. It's a lunatic, it stinks, it's got fleas and we have NO ROOM for it."

Behind her back, Lily pulled out Gerry's stopper and squeezed and squeezed to

80

squash the air out of him.

"And that goes for you too, Sammy," said Nick the Chippie. "You're grounded too."

Sammy groaned. "But I've only just got here!" He fixed Tiger Lily with an angry glare. "Thanks, Tiger! I'm giving you A BLACK SPOT!"

As the library van turned on to the main road, the warning bells of the level crossing were sounding and the barrier was coming down.

"Just our luck," Mum said, drumming her fingers on the steering wheel. "The 13:25." (The 13:25 was one of the two trains that stopped in The Middle of Nowhere every day.)

Tiger Lily could see Smoky Bacon, the

stationmaster, on the platform. He drew a large watch out of his waistcoat pocket and looked anxiously up and down the line.

"Isn't he exactly like the White Rabbit in *Alice in Wonderland*?" she remarked. "You know, *I'm late, I'm late for a very important date...*"

"Shut up, Tiger!" said Sammy.

"Don't be SILLY, Lily!" said Mum.

"Spot on, Tiger!" said Nick, and he grinned at her over his shoulder.

❀   ❀   ❀

Captain's Log
May 22nd

13:00   Set sail once more for The Middle of Nowhere. Steering problems. River flowing in the wrong direction.

13:15   Captain fell overboard. Hispaniola drifting. Order given to ABANDON SHIP.

Tiger Lily's Diary

22nd May 8pm

I don't believe it!

I have been grounded for the whole
week of the school holidays
even though I was the one
who got soaked and bitten
alive. So much for being a
Knight Errant roaming the
world in search of adventure.

Now I will NEVER be
able to become a heroine
because I will be stuck here
where absolutely nothing
happens EVER!

Things to do

1. Dog Shampoo (ask Auntie Pamela)
2. Buy flea collar
3. Look for dog-training book in the library

Chapter 8

"So, Tiger," said Auntie Pamela, "you're grounded."

"Yes, and it's not fair. Mum is still mad. Every time she sees me she says A PALLET! What I want to know is – who was the SNITCH who saw us on the river and told. I bet it was Sweetness and Light. They saw me with the bin liner."

"Now, don't go jumping to conclusions!" said Pamela sharply. "Let sleeping dogs lie."

"People shouldn't stick their wolf noses into other people's business."

"Calm down, Lily. We're all in enough trouble. Your mum already blames me and Granny for not keeping an eye on you. And PLEASE don't say anything to her about her hair when she comes back."

"What happened to her hair?"

"She had to rush off with the foil things still in, when she got the call about you on the river, and then the dye was in too long and then, well, these things happen. You can't really see the bald bit at the back. Not really. But seriously, Tiger, that raft idea has to be your maddest brainwave yet."

Lily gave her an embarrassed, lopsided grin. It was Sunday morning and Auntie Pamela had dropped round to use the printer. Tiger Lily was downloading bookplates from the internet to stick in all her old second-hand library books where the library stamp pages had been torn out. Her mum was having a driving lesson.

"Talking of sleeping dogs..." Auntie Pamela dropped her voice to a whisper, "...what are you going to do about the mad mutt?"

"Rosie? I'm going to keep her."

At the mention of her name, Rosie stuck her head out from under the table where she was thoughtfully munching a book. She thumped her tail and poked furiously at an itch behind her shoulder.

"Auntie Pamela, would nit shampoo kill dog fleas?"

"No!" said Pamela. "Why? Has she got fleas? Have you got nits?" She hastily whizzed across the room on the swivel chair and said brightly to change the subject, "What do you think of my poster?"

86

OPENING OF THE NEW COMMUNITY CENTRE

LET'S MAKE MIDSUMMER NIGHT AT THE OLD JAM FACTORY A NIGHT TO REMEMBER!

Come to the BAY TREE CAFÉ this Tuesday 7.30 pm with your suggestions to celebrate the opening of our new Community Centre.

ALL WELCOME

"I was thinking you might like to dance or sing a song or something…"

Tiger Lily gasped. "You mean, on a proper stage?"

Already she could see her name in lights; she would have a dressing-room with a huge mirror surrounded by spotlights and bouquets of flowers from well-wishers and paparazzi with flashing cameras waiting for her at the stage door.

"And to think it all started," she murmured dreamily, "in the Old Jam Factory."

"What all started in the Old Jam Factory?" Mum was back. She came in wearing an enormous multi-coloured woolly hat. Tiger Lily opened her mouth to say something and closed it again.

Pam waved the poster. "Have a look! It's about the meeting to plan the Midsummer Night concert at the Old Jam Factory. What do you think?"

"What do I think? I think that Midsummer Night is just one month away, Pam. Far be it from me to throw cold water on your plans – I know that you love singing – but there is NO WAY that building is going to be ready."

"Oh yes there is! Streaky has taken on a new Polish guy. He's going to work full-time,

painting the factory." Pamela looked deeply into her coffee cup. "He's lovely," she said dreamily.

"What Polish guy?" Tiger Lily's ears pricked up. "Is his name Piotr? Does he play the flute?"

"That's right. He's going to be my lodger while he's living here."

"He's what?" said Mum. "When were you talking to him? Is he the guy that…" At that moment, Auntie Pamela started making funny choking noises and rolling her eyes and Mum had to thump her back several times before she could catch her breath again.

"The Pied Piper is going to live here?" Tiger Lily kept shouting above the coughing. "I have to tell Sammy IMMEDIATELY."

90

Tiger Lily

"STOP, TIGER! Come back. Remember, you're grounded."

And to her mum's surprise, Tiger Lily sat down again without a murmur and gave her a big winning smile.

"You called me Tiger!"

Her mum groaned and poured herself a cup of coffee.

From:	Tiger Lily
Date:	Sun 23 May
To:	Sammy
Subject:	Wolves

Hiya,

Please call at my house tomorrow morning at nine o'clock precisely. There are Wolves in the village spying on us. DO NOT RING THE DOORBELL. Just meow loudly three times.

Tiger Lily

PS The Pied Piper is staying at my Auntie Pamela's! He will be at the café on Tuesday night. I will explain all.

Chapter 9

The following morning, just after the nine o'clock pips on the radio, Tiger Lily heard a faint "meow-meow" on the street outside followed immediately by two louder ones "MEOW-MEOW MEOW-MEOW".

She silently slipped out of the house, with Rosie limping after her. As long as she was back before Mum was out of the shower, no one would ever know.

Sammy was waiting for her with Zog. "I don't know why I can't just ring the doorbell like a normal person," Sammy grumbled.

Love You
sweetie

"Because," Tiger explained patiently, "we're grounded. And secondly, that's the way Huck Finn does it."

Sammy rolled his eyes. "Well, excuse me, *honey child*."

Tiger Lily narrowed her eyes. "We're not doing that today. First we are going to the post office. Then I will tell you about the Pied Piper and the Midsummer Night concert."

"Why are we going to the post office? I'm supposed to be doing my homework."

Tiger lowered her voice conspiratorially. "The Wolf twins have been spying on us. Now, I fear Sweetness is going to murder Light."

"Sweetness is going to murder Light?" Sammy yelped.

"Or Light is going to murder Sweetness. Whichever. Either way, we may not have much time. I've just read a book about twins. Have you ever heard of Romulus and Remus?"

"No," said Sammy, "but I expect you're going to tell me."

Tiger Lily's Book Reports
As told to her trusty companion, Sammy.

The Story of Romulus and Remus

Romulus and Remus were twin baby princes but their cruel uncle threw them into the river Tiber so that he could be the king but they were rescued by a SHE-WOLF. When they grew up, they decided to build a town of their own near the place where the she-wolf saved them. But this is the best bit. Remus jeered at Romulus and said the wall he was building was too low and he leaped over it to prove it. Romulus was so furious that he KILLED him. The city that Romulus founded is called Rome.

I think they had such bad tempers because:
1. they grew up in a WOLF family
2. they had been thrown into the river
3. their father was Mars, the god of war.

I give it: 5 she-wolves

Sweetness and Light's shop was very easy to miss unless you knew it was there, for it didn't look at all like a proper shop. It had two small grimy windows with pots of dusty blue hydrangeas dying on the window sills.

Tiger Lily peered into the gloom through one of the dirty panes. Sweetness (or was it Light?) was sitting at the right-hand end of the counter under the clock, sewing something. Her sister was at the other end beside the weighing scales, looking in the

opposite direction, also sewing. With their backs to one another, they looked like two bookends. Two grey bookends with sharp noses and black velvet berets.

"Do you see the way they're sitting?" Tiger pointed. "They clearly detest one another. Sooner or later, one of them will hop over that counter and brain the other one with a rolling pin. It's the wolf in them."

"Blimey!" said Sammy. He nudged Lily. "Look, cats."

And, indeed, there were cats. There were at least five, including Tango the station cat, snoozing on a battered old leather sofa, and two more on the counter. Zog and Rosie were whimpering and dribbling so much with excitement that Sammy had to tie them to a railing on Railway Street before Tiger Lily dared open the door.

"Hello," she said brightly, trying hard not to breathe in the smell of cat pee.

The sisters looked suspiciously down their long sharp identical noses at her.

It seemed very rude to accuse them straight away of being spies, not to mention would-be murderers, so Tiger Lily gazed around at the bare shelves to give herself time to think.

Sammy cautiously lifted the rusty lid of the freezer. He would not have been at all surprised to find a dead wolf lying in there, but instead there was only a spilt packet of frozen peas and a frost-burned tray of pork chops.

"Do you sell jam?" said Lily suddenly. "I'm looking for jam!"

"No jam today," said Sweetness through her small tight mouth.

"Will there be jam tomorrow?" Lily smiled politely at Light.

"Jam is my sister Sophia's department," Light replied, looking at her through her small grey eyes. "She deals with jam."

"In that case, we'll have…" Tiger Lily peered dubiously into a crate of wrinkled vegetables which might have been elderly carrots or turnips or, possibly, parsnips.

"Vegetables are my sister Lydia's department," said Sweetness.

The post office clock ticked loudly.

Light was standing poised over the vegetable crate waiting for Tiger Lily to speak when suddenly the shop door was thrown violently open and in burst Rosie and Zog, barking at the top of their voices.

The cats were awake in an instant. They leaped off the sofa and scattered in every direction with Rosie and Zog in hot pursuit. Sweetness and Light were both screaming "Help!" and "Stop that!" and "Get out of here, you rascals!" and "No,

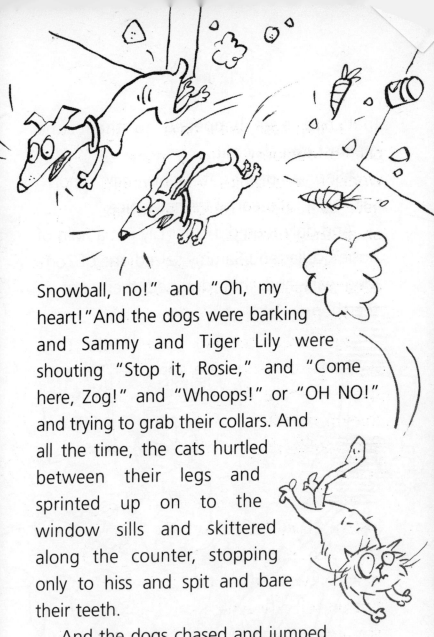

Snowball, no!" and "Oh, my
heart!" And the dogs were barking
and Sammy and Tiger Lily were
shouting "Stop it, Rosie," and "Come
here, Zog!" and "Whoops!" or "OH NO!"
and trying to grab their collars. And
all the time, the cats hurtled
between their legs and
sprinted up on to the
window sills and skittered
along the counter, stopping
only to hiss and spit and bare
their teeth.

And the dogs chased and jumped
and BARKED as if this was the very best thing

that had ever happened to them, the greatest ever day out.

"Sophia, dear, get Smoky next door!" said Light in a tearful trembly voice.

And only then did Tiger Lily get a hold of Rosie's collar and Sammy seized one of Zog's long ears and they dragged them out of the shop.

Chapter 10

Smoky was on the phone to Mum before Tiger Lily had even turned into One-End Street.

"Lily Larkin! What am I going to do with you? The poor Wolfs. This is UNFORGIVABLE."

Tiger Lily tried to explain that it was all a terrible mistake. "We didn't go to frighten them deliberately. I'm really really sorry," she pleaded. "I just had this idea that one of the twins might kill the other one, you know, because they were brought up by wolves like Romulus and Remus."

"Romulus and Remus?" repeated Mum. "Don't be so SILLY, Lily. You mustn't let your imagination run away with you. They're just a pair of poor shy little ladies who wouldn't say boo to a goose. You know something? I blame myself. I have filled your head with stories from the day you were born. And what has happened? Reading is making you mad!" They both surveyed the kitchen with its teetering piles of books. "And furthermore, young lady, that stinking flea-bitten dog of yours is chewing books. I want it out of the house. FOR GOOD!"

Lily's lip trembled. She had a big lump in her throat.

"I'm going upstairs," said Mum. "Do

anything you like but DO NOT READ! I am taking you to Granny's for lunch and you must STAY there until I come to the meeting this evening. You are DOUBLE GROUNDED. Is that clear?"

"Yes, Mum."

Tiger Lily crawled under the table. Rosie was sleeping with her head resting on a thick blue book. She looked so sweet and vulnerable, it was hard to imagine that anyone could have abandoned her.

"Come on, Rosie, give me the book."

Lily slid the book out from under her. It was slightly damp and pulpy. "Stories from Shakespeare", it said on the cover in fine gold letters.

Tiger looked up at the ceiling. Nothing stirred in the house. Mum was still upstairs. Her last instruction "DO NOT READ!" was still ringing in Lily's ears but she couldn't help it.

She opened the book.

"Wow!"

There was a play called *A Midsummer Night's Dream*! It was definitely A SIGN. She had to read it.

The most excellent thing about *A Midsummer Night's Dream* was that it had fairies and kings and queens and star-crossed lovers and actors and love potions and loads of heroines and

106

loads of music and it all happened on Midsummer Night. Some of the characters had unpronounceable names like Hippolyta which sounded like some sort of food for a hippopotamus on a diet, and some had really funny names like Flute and Bottom but, Tiger Lily thought, what could be more perfect for the opening of the Old Jam Factory than *A Midsummer Night's Dream* on Midsummer Night.

Especially as Auntie Pamela and the Pied Piper could be one of the star-crossed couples, and there was a very good part for Sammy. *And I*, she thought dreamily, *I shall be Titania, Queen of the Fairies*.

And she absent-mindedly picked up a wooden spoon for a wand and spread a little fairy dust around the kitchen.

From: Tiger Lily
Date: Tuesday 13:04:25
To: Sammy
Subject: Meeting tonight

Hi Sammy,
I am in terrible trouble. Are you? Did your dad tell you about the Midsummer Night concert? Are you coming to the meeting tonight? I have a FANTASTIC plan.

Tiger

Not if I can help it.

Sammy

From: Sammy
Date: Tuesday 14:44:11
To: Lily Larkin
Subject: Re: Meeting tonight

The Bay Tree Café

TODAY'S SPECIALS

Porridge Goldilocks

Bacon Rolls (absolutely not Wilbur or Babe)

Omelette Humpty-Dumpty – a cracking good choice

Rita's Legendary Bean Soup – food for heroes

Pizza Pinocchio – a runaway success – TRUE!

Long John Silver's Pirate Pie

Queen of Hearts Jam Tarts

Blyton Mess – strawberries with cream and crushed meringue

Chapter 11

By 7.30 that evening, the Bay Tree Café was packed to the rafters. Lily was still in disgrace so she sat at the back, trying to look invisible, and redesigned the Bay Tree Café menu. Granny had allowed her to sneak in Rosie as long as she kept her out of sight.

Sammy had come after all with his dad but wouldn't catch her eye. Everyone else sat about drinking tea until Auntie Pamela arrived with a clipboard tucked under her arm.

She was just introducing the Pied Piper –
"I'd like you all to say hello to the multi-
talented Piotr," she smiled, "who has so
kindly agreed to be our Musical Director…"
– when a deep voice boomed from the
doorway:

"WE PROTEST!"

Everybody swivelled around.

Mr and Mrs Hannibal from Hannibals' farm were standing in the doorway. Side by side, they looked as wide as their own barn door and as terrifying as their Highland bull. They stomped into the café in their mucky wellingtons, bringing with them the pungent whiff of wet goat and hairy cattle.

Granny Rita raised an eyebrow. "Protest about what exactly?"

"About this Midsummer Concert. If any of you ever bothered to read the local newspaper and find out what is going on under your own noses, you'd know we have been planning on having a bonfire…"

"…with a goat-roast…"

Sammy stuck a finger in his mouth and made pretend retching noises until Granny Rita gave him one of her hard stares.

"…and we don't see why you have to go and choose the ONE night in the WHOLE year to open this … this so-called Community Centre…" The Hannibals cut a swathe through the tables and chairs until they were right beside Pamela. Mr Hannibal jabbed his finger at her face and roared, "…when it is hard enough to make a living from farming … is it too much to ask for a LITTLE bit of local support?" His face had turned brick red and his finger kept jabbing and jabbing and jabbing.

Auntie Pamela shrank back.

There was a sharp intake of breath from everyone in the café.

Under Lily's chair, Rosie bravely bared her teeth.

The Pied Piper lightly touched Mr Hannibal's sleeve.

"Please, sir," he said, "don't speak like that to Pamela."

Hannibal shrugged his arm away. They eyeballed one another. Tiger Lily held her breath.

Would Hannibal thump the Pied Piper?

Would the Pied Piper thump Hannibal?

Nobody moved.

"Whoa!" said Streaky Bacon, sounding braver than he felt. "Let's all calm down here. Who said this Midsummer Night concert was going to happen anyway?"

"Excuse me?" Auntie Pamela smiled at Streaky through gritted teeth.

"Sorry, Pam, but the Jam Factory is probably, that is to say, at the end of the day, when all is said and done, taking into account, and factoring in all the variables…"

"What are you trying to say?"

"It won't be ready for Midsummer Night."

"NOT READY?" everyone chorused.

Streaky stretched his neck like a goose about to take flight, rubbed an index finger under his collar as if it was choking him, and jabbed at Spanners Murphy's shoulder. "You tell them."

Spanners Murphy rose reluctantly to his feet and coughed.

"You see, folks, we're having a few problems with the old plumbing." He mumbled stuff about sprinkler systems and central heating boilers and old lead piping.

"Meaning?" Auntie Pamela's elegant polished nails drummed on her clipboard.

Spanners tugged at an earlobe. "Sorry,

Pam, but Streaky – and me too – well, we think you should postpone the concert till later in the year…"

There was a stunned silence until Auntie Pamela spluttered, "But we can't cancel

now. Piotr and I..." for some reason, she turned a little red, "...we have planned the music. We're giving a performance of baroque songs with flute accompaniment."

"And I've already planned the menu for supper afterwards," said Granny.

"AND I," Lily shouted (she had climbed up on her chair to make herself heard above the din), "I am going to direct and star in *A Midsummer Night's Dream* by Mr William Shakespeare... I have parts for all of you."

"You're WHAT?" said Mum, who had just arrived.

"*A Midsummer Night's Dream*. It's perfect! I'm going to be Titania, the Queen of the Fairies and you can be Hippolyta and Sammy is going to be Bottom."

"Don't be SILLY, Lily. We don't have the time to rehearse a whole play," her mum protested, but Sammy cut her off.

"TIGER!" he yelled. "You CANNOT BE SERIOUS! First you make me a SLAVE and then you make me a WRETCHED CABIN

118

BOY and then you nearly WASH ME OUT TO SEA and now you expect me to be someone called BOTTOM?"

"It's all right, Sammy," said Tiger Lily soothingly, "he's very funny. He has a donkey's head and I put a chain of flowers around his neck."

"NO WAY! I RESIGN," Sammy shouted. "I'm not going to be your trusty companion any more. All you do is get me into trouble."

Rosie did not like seeing her beloved Tiger under attack. She bounced out from her hiding place, baring her teeth and making strange throaty noises.

Mum thumped the counter. "That's it! Lily, will you PLEASE take that blinking dog out of here AT ONCE. Doesn't anyone here obey any rules at all?" She pointed at the NO DOGS notice on the door and glared at

Granny. "As the concert is cancelled, I suggest we might as well adjourn this meeting."

And she grabbed Lily by the elbow and marched her out of the café.

Tiger's Diary

Tuesday evening

Things have got worse. Not only am I grounded but I am not getting any pocket money because of what happened in Sweetness and Light's shop. Rosie has been locked in the shed. My trusty companion has resigned. My mother has banned me from reading. And the Midsummer Night concert is off.

Chapter 12

The following morning, Tiger Lily and Rosie tramped with heavy hearts to the Bay Tree Café. Her mother was still furious with her. She had called her expedition IRRESPONSIBLE. And said that what had happened in Sweetness and Light's shop was UNFORGIVABLE and that putting on *A Midsummer Night's Dream* was SILLY. And that Rosie HAD TO GO.

Lily sighed. Grown-ups were so SELFISH. That concert was the first good thing to happen in the village and they had to go and

Community Centre

cancel it. And all because of that muppet Streaky Bacon.

At the corner of Cannery Row, Tiger stopped. She could hear drumming. Very loud drumming coming from Nick the Chippie's barn at the bottom of the road.

Tiger Lily bit her lip. *Perhaps it was a bit rude to ask Sammy to be Bottom*, she thought, forgetting that she had never actually asked him at all. She had just blurted out her plan without even talking to him about it. She sighed. It was no wonder he had resigned as her trusty companion. Especially as it was her fault that he was grounded.

While Tiger Lily was thinking these depressing thoughts, she and Rosie had

Opening Soon

followed their noses and walked up to the Old Jam Factory where the Pied Piper was taking down the "Opening Soon" banner.

"Cześć," he said. "That means 'Hello' in Polish."

"Cześć," repeated Lily. "You know, if you really were the Pied Piper and you were going to play your flute, no one would dare cancel the concert because you would be a celebrity and the papers would be coming and maybe the television too, and Spanners would just have to get the plumbing fixed in time."

"I suppose so," agreed Piotr, "but I am not a famous person."

It was then that Tiger Lily had one of her ideas.

She *had* to talk to Nick the Chippie.

So that she wouldn't get into more trouble for wandering about the village while she was grounded, she persuaded Granny to

lock up the café and walk down to the Salvage Barn with her. Sammy was still playing his drums.

While Granny graciously listened to Sammy explaining why he needed something called a new hi-hat, Tiger went out to the yard where Nick the Chippie was sanding a garden bench.

"Nick," she said, "did you really play in the band with Paul Mann?"

"I sure did," said Nick, "though that was in the days before he started to Save the World."

Tiger Lily told him her plan.

Chapter 13

"Paul Mann is coming to open the Old Jam Factory?" Streaky exclaimed. "Why didn't you say? We'll get that plumbing seen to right away."

"Paul Mann is coming to open the Old Jam Factory?" exclaimed Mr and Mrs Hannibal. "Why didn't you say? What a super idea! On our behalf, would you invite him and the whole village to our goat-roast and bonfire AFTER the concert. Will the press be coming?"

"Of course," said Tiger Lily, grinning.

"Paul Mann is coming to open the Old Jam Factory?" Auntie Pamela screamed. "Why didn't you say? I must start rehearsing at once."

Half a dozen phone calls later and Tiger Lily looked like the cat that had eaten all the cream. The Midsummer Night Concert was back on.

"So," said Sammy, with a very long and flamboyant drum roll, "it's all SORTED!"

"Yes," said Tiger, "so could we please do a teeny weeny bit of *A Midsummer Night's Dream*?"

Sammy shot her a warning look.

"You don't have to be Bottom," she explained hurriedly. "You can be Puck. He's the most important person in the whole play. Swear. Cross my heart. Everyone will love you. Let me tell you all about it."

Sammy tapped out a four note rhythm on his bass drum. "Oh go on then," he said.

Tiger Lily's Book Reports
As told to her trusty companion, Sammy.

A Midsummer Night's Dream
by William Shakespeare.

This play takes place in a forest in Greece. It can make you dizzy at first trying to work out who is in love with who – and who should be in love with who – because everyone is always in the wrong place in the forest with the wrong person and a really funny fairy called PUCK, that's you, keeps putting magic potions on their eyelids while they are asleep so that they fall in love with the first person they see when they wake up. There is an actor called BOTTOM who has a donkey's head and the fairy queen TITANIA, that's me, falls in love with him because of the eyelid juice trick.

At the end all the right people are together and PUCK, that's you, makes the last really important speech.

I give it: 5 Fairy Queens wearing crowns

"OK, I'll be in the play," said Sammy, "as long as I can do a drum duo with Paul Mann as well."

Tiger Lily looked at Nick. Nick stroked his chin. "We'd better start practising then, Sam."

Mum agreed that Lily could visit Sweetness and Light that evening when she told her that she had to Redress a Wrong.

As soon as she opened the shop door, the twins scuttled behind the counter and clutched each other's hands, looking nervously over Tiger Lily's shoulder to see if she had brought the dog. She hadn't.

"What do you want?" said Sweetness anxiously (or maybe it was Light).

"Please leave us alone!" said Light (or maybe it was Sweetness).

"Actually," Tiger Lily began in a rush, "I have come to apologize and to give you a pot of raspberry jam that my granny made and, well," she slowed down, "the main reason I am here is to ask for your help."

"Our help?" said Sweetness and Light together. They stood up.

"I thought you might like to be the dressers at the Midsummer Night concert. Since you are both such good sewers and you always wear such nice clothes. And you could help make a fairy costume for me and the costume for Puck and whatever the wieners are going to wear... If you are not too busy."

Sweetness looked at Light. Light looked back at Sweetness.

"Thank you very much," said Sweetness.

"We would like that very much," said Light.

And they smiled!

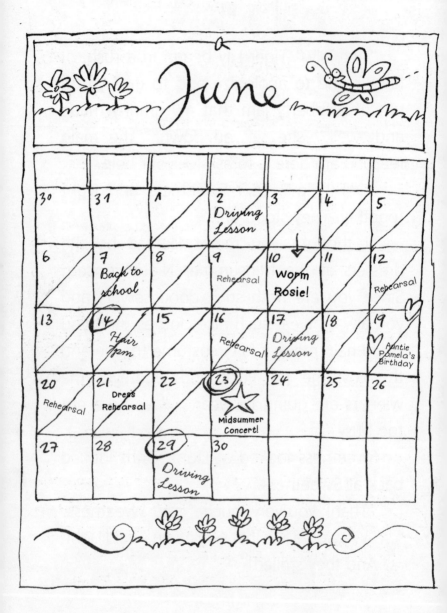

Tiger Lily's Diary

20th June

Busy, busy, busy!

All month, I have been learning my lines and
going to rehearsals and practising my
dance routines and designing the programme for the
concert. Sammy comes every weekend to rehearse with
me and practise his drumming with his dad.

The Pied Piper is teaching all the wieners to play
"Oh when the saints go marching in" on the recorder.
Sweetness and Light are making me a brilliant
costume.

I have a TIARA! I have WINGS!

I can't believe how excited everyone is about
Paul Mann coming. Smoky Bacon has already
put up hundreds of hanging baskets in the station!
The Pied Piper has invited all his Polish friends to come
from the city. Streaky Bacon has started wearing
sunglasses and a leather waistcoat. Granny is
practising making sushi because it's supposed
to be Paul Mann's favourite food. Nick
the Chippie says "Everything will be all
right on the night" but I don't know.
Just look at this newspaper cutting!

Rock Legend in The Middle of Nowhere!

International rock legend and Peace Campaigner, Paul Mann (38), will be making a rare appearance in The Middle of Nowhere when he arrives to re-open the Old Jam Factory as a Community Centre on Midsummer Night. He comes at the invitation of Nick "The Chippie" of the Salvage Barn, who was the drummer in Mann's first band, Mann's People.

According to Stationmaster "Smoky" Bacon (64), extra train carriages will be laid on for the many hundreds of Mann's fans who are expected to turn up...

I spoke to one of the few children who live in The Middle of Nowhere. Lily Larkin (10), known as Tiger to her friends, blushed when I asked her if it had really been her idea to invite Paul Mann. "Well yes, but I never thought he was going to turn up. It's unbelievable. It's like a dream!"

Chapter 14

Streaky Bacon kept saying "It will be all right on the night" too, but everything was not all right at all. With only hours to go before Paul Mann's arrival, Spanners Murphy was still mooching around backstage with a bag of spanners and wrenches.

"Just a few last-minute details, Streaky, don't fret. Keep your hair on," he drawled. "I've had to turn off the water again."

Tiger Lily couldn't stay still. She nervously pirouetted between the hall and the square, scattering fairy dust for good luck.

Sammy stood on tiptoes at the corner of Cannery Row, like a meercat, watching out for Paul Mann's limousine. Granny and Mum were busy laying a strip of red carpet that they had borrowed from the church. Milo and Streaky Junior were getting in everyone's way practising their break-dance routines.

Back in the hall, the Tooter Tots, the wieners' recorder group, were rehearsing on the main stage with the Pied Piper. Auntie Pamela was practising her scales, and to add to the din, Nick the Chippie was finishing something off with an electric sander.

Tiger Lily went to sit in the bay tree by herself.

Then the first catastrophe struck! A man phoned to say that the lorry that was supposed to deliver the seating had broken down. No, he couldn't say when they'd get through. He wasn't making any promises.

"How can we have a concert without seats?" Auntie Pamela wailed. "We can't make people sit on the floor. We shall have to cancel after all."

Tiger Lily was having none of it. As soon as the Tooters reached the last ear-splitting bar of "Oh When The Saints..." she spoke to the Pied Piper.

"Ingenious!" said Piotr. He picked up his flute and started to play. Tiger Lily and Sammy and the Tooter Tots and Milo Hannibal and Streaky Junior fell into line behind him like the children of Hamelin and Piotr led them tripping and skipping around the village.

They picked up deckchairs and white plastic patio seats from people's gardens. They brought back straight-backed dining-chairs and kitchen stools and swivelling desk chairs. Milo Hannibal and Streaky Junior panted up the hill with the old cracked leather, cat-pee-smelling sofa from

Sweetness and Light's shop. Auntie Pamela sent over a shampooing chair from Curl Up & Dye. Sammy's dad gave them a partially-stripped garden bench.

Mrs Hannibal volunteered a tractor load of straw bales.

Lily's mum watched dubiously as Tiger and Sammy struggled down the aisle with Granny's armchair.

"It all looks a bit higgledy-piggledy... There's going to be a lot of reporters and..."

"Nonsense. It's fantastic. Very Tigerish," said Auntie Pamela and Piotr together.

Mum frowned. "When did you two start talking like some sort of double act?"

And then, just as it looked as if everything was going to be fine after all, Nick the Chippie's mobile rang.

"It's Paul Mann," he said in a loud voice.

Tiger Lily's mouth went completely dry.

"Paul! That's great! Congratulations!" Nick said. Then his voice changed. "Oh no! That's too bad. Well, thanks for letting us know, mate." He rang off.

"What is it?" said Pamela. "What did he say?"

"He says he's sorry to disappoint us. He has to go to New York with the Prime Minister. They're getting some sort of peace prize." Nick didn't dare look at Tiger Lily.

"Well, that's it, people," Auntie Pamela said. "We might as well pack up. The show's definitely OFF. It was never meant to be. We'll try again when we have the proper seats ... and Paul Mann."

And, to Lily's disgust, all the grown-ups, except Sammy's dad, just stopped in the middle of whatever they were doing, shrugged their shoulders and WALKED OUT!

"Come back," Lily wailed, but nobody paid any attention.

Tiger Lily and Sammy slumped forlornly on Sweetness and Light's sofa. Milo swivelled in the desk chair. Streaky Junior tilted back in the shampooing chair. The Tooter Tots sat on the stage.

"It's not fair," said Sammy. "Some stupid trip to New York with the Prime Minister and Paul Mann thinks, 'Oh, The Middle of Nowhere, that's so uncool, forget it'."

"So what now, Tiger?" Nick asked.

Tiger Lily scowled. "This would never

happen in a book. In a book, the heroine would say, 'Let's put the show on Right Here!' and everyone would cheer and give high fives and shout 'Break a Leg' and 'See you on stage'!"

They all fell silent and had a think about this. Then Tiger Lily bounced up and waved her wand. "Who needs Paul Mann anyway? LET'S DO IT. TOOTER TOTS, STAND UP AND SMILE! THE SHOW IS GOING ON AND YOU'RE TOPPING THE BILL."

"Way to go, Tiger!" Nick gave a drum roll. "Let's call everyone back."

ON THE OCCASION OF THE OPENING OF THE

Old Jam Factory

in the absence of anybody important

TIGER LILY THEATRE PRODUCTIONS PRESENT

A Midsummer
Night's Concert

WITH A HOST OF DRAMATIC ENTERTAINMENTS,
MUSICAL DIVERTISSEMENTS, ACROBATS, TUMBLERS,
CHOIRS OF ANGELS, DRUMMERS, ILLUSIONISTS, AND
THE CELEBRATED PIED PIPER, NEWLY ARRIVED FROM
HIS TRIUMPHS IN HAMELIN, SIAM AND BAGHDAD.

WITH A SPECIAL APPEARANCE BY

Tiger Lily as Queen Titania
and
Sammy as Puck

THE ENTERTAINMENT WILL CONCLUDE WITH A
PHANTASMAGORICAL MIDSUMMER NIGHT SUPPER AT
THE BAY TREE CAFÉ AND A PYROTECHNICAL
EXTRAVAGANZA & BONFIRE AT THE UNIQUE RARE
BREEDS FARM AND RESIDENCE OF MR AND MRS
HANNIBAL.

DIRECTOR . . . . Pamela

DESIGNER . . . . Pamela

STAGE MANAGER . . . . Pamela

MUSICAL DIRECTOR . . . . Piotr

ASST. MUSICAL DIRECTOR . . . . Pamela

JOINT CATERING . . . . The Bay Tree Café

Hannibals' Farm

LIGHTING . . . . Sparks 'R' Us

SET CONSTRUCTION . . . . Nick the Chippie

WARDROBE SUPERVISORS . . . . . Sweetness and Light

TITANIA'S HAIR . . . . Pamela of Curl Up & Dye

SEATING . . . . Ingenious Solutions

PROGRAMME DESIGN . . . . Tiger Lily

THE VILLAGE WOULD LIKE TO THANK OUR SPONSORS,
BACON BUILDERS, WITHOUT WHOM THE OLD FACTORY
WOULD HAVE BEEN FINISHED MONTHS AGO.

Have a Great
Midsummer Night!

Chapter 15

First up onstage were the Tooter Tots. Sweetness and Light had dressed them in red tutus with silver paper scales sewn on their backs and shoulders. They went plinkety-plink on their xylophones, tinkled their triangles, squawked on their recorders and sang "We are little fishies, swimming all together". There was hardly a dry eye in the house.

Then, in the absence of Paul Mann, but with the hundreds of his fans who had arrived on the 19:14 train, Sammy and Nick

the Chippie did their drum duo, bouncing the rhythms back from one to the other like real rock stars.

The crowd loved it. "HURRAY, BRAVO!"

They leaped to their feet at the last bang and nearly raised the roof beams.

The man from *The Times*, who had been really huffy on account of nobody bothering to tell him that Paul Mann wasn't coming, even cheered up and took loads of photographs.

Nearly everyone had a part. Smoky Bacon did magic tricks that didn't work; Granny Rita tap-danced, Milo and Streaky Junior break-danced and Pamela and the Pied Piper did their baroque songs with flute accompaniment.

"And now," said Pamela, "to conclude, we have the pleasure of seeing Miss Tiger Lily, as Queen Titania, and Sammy as Puck, from the final scene of *A Midsummer Night's Dream*. After which…" Backstage, there was a fearsome thump followed by a terrible crash. Pamela shot a troubled look towards the wings and gabbled, "…we hope you'll all join us for supper in the square and a fireworks party at Hannibals' farm."

The lights dimmed. The Mann's People fans shifted around on their bottoms on the garden furniture and old sofas.

Then a single spotlight came on, creating a pool of midsummer-night yellow in the centre of the stage.

Sammy entered with a broom. He was wearing a blonde wig, a green hat, green tights and a fringed tunic – a cross between a rotund elf and Robin Hood.

" *Now the hungry lion roars,* " he began.

Everyone leaned forward in their seats to listen. Behind the back curtain, there was another loud thump and the sound of running feet.

" *And we fairies that do run... From the presence of the sun...* "

The hammering and rattling backstage grew louder. There was a rumbling and a roaring overhead. The stage lights flickered. Sammy raised his voice. "*Not a mouse shall disturb this hallowed house...*"

The audience couldn't help themselves. They roared with laughter.

Sammy paused and looked towards the wings where Pamela had made an unscheduled appearance.

She semaphored wildly at him and drew her hand across her throat in a cutting gesture.

"What?" he hissed.

"Cut! Cut!"

Sammy peered into the darkness of the auditorium, but blinded in his spotlight, saw nothing and continued.

"...*I am sent with broom before to sweep the dust behind the door.*"

The audience were in stitches, slapping their knees and stuffing their fists in their mouths.

Sammy fled into the wings with his sweeping broom where Sweetness and Light were buttoning Tiger Lily into her fairy dress and spangled wings ... and Mum was telling her she couldn't go on.

"What do you mean, I can't go on?"

"It's the plumbing. The boiler is going mad and all the pipes are shuddering. We're stopping the show. It's nearly over anyway."

"No, it isn't." Lily's lip trembled. "I still have to do Titania's speech and bless the new theatre.

Everybody has had a part except me."

Mum hesitated.

"She's right," said Sweetness, straightening the wings on Tiger Lily's back and placing her star wand in her hand.

"She's right," insisted Light, placing her fairy tiara on Tiger Lily's head and pushing her out on to the stage.

"Break a leg!" said Sammy.

Out of sight, Piotr's flute played magic fairy dance music.

Tiger Lily Queen Titania walked to the centre of the stage and curtsied.

153

She had just got to the bit "*Hand in hand with fairy grace...*" when she felt the first drops of water.

A flicker of doubt raced across her face. She looked up at the flies. The spotlights sputtered and went out. From somewhere deep in the bowels of the theatre, a slow rumble had started up, growing in momentum like a tropical storm. In the dark space in front of her, she could hear chairs being pushed back. There were murmurs, then screams. A baby howled.

" ...*Hand in hand with fairy grace*," she repeated, "*will we sing and bless this place...*"

And then, suddenly, water was pouring out of the ceiling with the full force of a summer deluge – the sprinkler system had burst.

Pamela's disembodied voice crackled over the sound system. "Will everyone please make your way calmly towards the exits? There is no need to panic. Please proceed calmly."

The audience, like a frightened herd of wildebeest, stampeded towards the exit. In the rush, Pamela tripped and lost a shoe. The fire curtain dropped like a stone. Tiger Lily was left alone on the stage in the dark, dripping in her sodden fairy costume when someone yanked her arm.

"Come on," shouted the Pied Piper,

throwing her over his shoulder in a fireman's lift.

They emerged dripping into the square to the sound of fire engines wailing. Lily's white make-up was streaked with rivulets of black eyeliner and angry tears. She had lost her wand and her tiara.

"You look like a panda," Sammy told her.

Chapter 16

Later, when the firemen had left and the sprinkler system had been disconnected, Auntie Pamela locked up the Jam Factory and the Midsummer Night party got under way.

It was still bright and the square looked fantastic. Granny Rita had set up trestle tables, groaning with sushi and salads and crab claws and pizza Pinocchio. The Hannibals had a stand with kidburgers ("Not bad," Sammy admitted) and Midsummer Night Magic Potion, which was really raspberry milkshake. In honour of Piotr and all his Polish friends, Auntie Pamela had bought pierogi and poppy seed cake and herrings with raw onions.

"Well, it's only fair after all the work he has done," she said, blushing.

"Take it easy on that Midsummer Night Magic Potion, Pam," Granny Rita told her, "it's strong stuff."

Tiger Lily was not at the party. She sat close to tears in the fork of the bay tree, invisible, unmissed by everyone. Rosie lay on the ground beneath her, her long face resting on her good front foot. "Woe is me!" she whispered. "What a fiasco! Everyone is sniggering about

me. I shall have to run away and join a travelling circus. If only I had some rich relation to leave me a fortune unexpectedly; then I could go to Paris or Buenos Aires and come back home as My Lady Something and everybody who laughed at me would be sorry but I wouldn't be at all hoity-toity. I would forgive them all and people would say—"

"Lily."

Tiger Lily peered through the glossy thicket of leaves.

Jim the slave, the Pied Piper, Cinderella, Romulus and Remus and Marmee all peered back at her. She rubbed her eyes and the faces of Sammy, Piotr, Auntie Pamela, Sweetness & Light and Mum swam back into focus.

Her eyes welled up. "I'm not Huckleberry Finn, or the boy with the limp who got left behind to tell the Pied Piper story. I'm not Cinderella's Fairy Godmother, or the She-Wolf who rescued Romulus and Remus, or Jo March, or even Queen Titania. I'm just me."

"Lily?" Mum repeated.

"What do you want?"

"Just come down."

Lily's sparkly silver shoes appeared first, then her long legs in their white tights, then Queen Titania's fairy dress with the wings crestfallen and looking somewhat the worse for the soaking and, last of all, her make-up-streaked long face.

"Here she is, ladies and gentlemen." Piotr tapped a glass with his baton to call everyone to order. "Our Midsummer Night Star."

"I'm not a star," Tiger Lily sniffed. "I never do anything right."

"Oh yes, you do," said Sammy. "You invented the Pallet-Raft and went a-Roaming."

"And if you hadn't done that, I would not have found a job and a new home and…" Piotr looked starry-eyed at Pamela – for some reason, he was holding one of her shoes – "…your auntie."

"I don't understand," Lily sniffed.

"That day we met, I was worried about how you'd get back here so I walked to the station and told Smoky that I had seen you on the river…" Piotr explained.

"Smoky rang Streaky...

...Streaky went to the café and told your Granny Rita..."

"So I rang Pamela to see if you were with her..." said Granny.

"...And I was in the salon," said Mum, "getting my roots done ... so I rang Sammy's dad and we went to find you..."

"... And, meanwhile, Streaky offered me a job..."

"So, you were the snitch all the time?"

"Snitch? No, what was that word? I was

162

your *benefactor*, like Magwitch..."

"And you're obviously my Fairy Godmother!" Pamela gave Lily a wink as she accepted her shoe from Piotr, "for you found Prince Charming!"

Tiger Lily was flabbergasted. The Pied Piper was the Snitch AND her benefactor AND Prince Charming.

"And, remember," Sweetness and Light said together, "how you bravely Redressed a Wrong and gave us our lovely job."

Their noses no longer looked sharp enough to cut cheese. Maybe butter.

"And it was you who Saved the Day when the seating didn't arrive," said Mum.

"And you said the Show Must Go On when Paul Mann didn't come!" said the Tooter Tots.

Tiger Lily suddenly turned bright red.

"Well," said Nick, "are you going to tell everyone or am I?"

Tiger Lily gave everyone a crooked smile. "We didn't invite Paul Mann. He was never going to come to The Middle of Nowhere. We just SAID that he was, so that everyone would get on with organizing the concert."

"Lily!" Mum clapped her hands to her mouth.

"What?" spluttered Sammy. "I only said I would be Puck if I could do a drum duo with him."

Streaky Bacon looked dazed. "But all that overtime I paid—"

"And the money I've spent on sushi!" said Granny Rita.

"But then," Lily rushed on, "it nearly all went wrong again when Sammy's dad got the pretend phone call ... and you all walked out."

"Until you said the Show Must Go On," said Pamela and Piotr together.

"What a cunning plan!" said the man from *The Times*. "If there is any justice in the world, I'll get this story on the front page, Paul Mann or no Paul Mann. I think you're ingenious."

"So do we," shouted Sweetness and Light in their high reedy voices. "So hip, hip, hurray for Lily Larkin."

"Hip, hip, hurray," shouted everyone.

Rosie the three-legged greyhound didn't say anything. She just gazed up adoringly at Tiger Lily with soft wet eyes, but if you can understand Dog, you would know that the look meant: "You're wonderful. I was abandoned and you found me. I worship the ground you walk on."

Smoky Bacon, the stationmaster, cleared his throat. "I'd also like to say thank you to Tiger Lily. She certainly put The Middle of Nowhere on the map today. I've been rushed off my feet, checking tickets and giving out information about connections and watering my begonias and I'd love to stay and chat, but, oh dear," he pulled his watch out of his waistcoat pocket, "we're going to be late for the bonfire," and he trotted off across the square, calling everyone to follow him.

Tiger Lily looked around for Sammy. She found him at the buffet table spearing meatballs two at a time with a fork.

"Sammy?" she said.

"What?"

"Will you still be my trusty companion when you come back in the summer?"

167

Sammy swallowed at least six meatballs before answering.

"OK, Tiger," he mumbled, "I will be your companion on your night errands, but I refuse one hundred per cent to be a slave or a bottom or a wretched cabin boy. And no more sneaky tricks like that about Paul Mann. AND I am not wearing tights ever again. Especially green ones."

"It's Knight Errant," Tiger Lily corrected him, "like the Knights of the Round Table, roaming the world in search of adventure…"

"That's what I said," said Sammy, though

it was hard to make out exactly what he was saying because he was talking with his mouth full.

"Come on," said Piotr, "let's go and see this bonfire." And he took Auntie Pamela by the arm.

"*Give me your hands, if we be friends, my proud Titania,*" Mum said to Tiger Lily. "That's a quotation, Tiger."

"I know, Mum."

And she grinned because that was only the second time in her whole life that her mother had called her Tiger.

Arm in arm, they fell in beside Piotr and Auntie Pamela and joined the procession out of the square and down to Hannibals' farm, with Rosie and Zog and Sammy and Nick the Chippie and the Tooter Tots and Sweetness and Light and Spanners Murphy and Granny Rita and the Bacons and Piotr's Polish pals and all of Paul Mann's cheering fans.

And fireworks whistled up into the sky and fell back to earth in a multicoloured shower over Tiger Lily's head.

"Mum," she said, "about Rosie…"

NIGHT OF DRAMA AT THE OLD JAM FACTORY!

TIGER LILY BRINGS THE HOUSE DOWN

Find out more
about the author at

www.maevefriel.com